Exotic Pizza Murder

Book Nine

in

Papa Pacelli's

Pizzeria Series

By

Patti Benning

Author's Note: On the next page, you'll find out how to access all of my books easily, as well as locate books by best-selling author, Summer Prescott. I'd love to hear your thoughts on my books, the storylines, and anything else that you'd like to comment on – reader feedback is very important to me. Please see the following page for my publisher's contact information. If you'd like to be on her list of "folks to contact" with updates, release and sales notifications, etc…just shoot her an email and let her know. Thanks for reading!

Also…

…if you're looking for more great reads, from me and Summer, check out the Summer Prescott Publishing Book Catalog:

http://summerprescottbooks.com/book-catalog/ for some truly delicious stories.

TABLE OF CONTENTS

EXOTIC PIZZA

MURDER

Book Nine in Papa Pacelli's Pizzeria Series

CHAPTER ONE

Eleanora Pacelli set a tray down on one of the metal outdoor tables that had just been delivered. The tray was laden with glasses of fresh lemonade and a plate of brownie bites.

"Thanks, Ms. Pacelli. You really didn't have to."

"Nonsense, Sam, you and your men have been working so hard." Ellie grinned. "Besides, I need someone to test out the lemonade. It's my grandmother's recipe, and I'd like to begin selling it this summer."

"No complaints from us. We're happy to be guinea pigs." He gestured the other men over, and they each grabbed a glass.

While the workers took their break, Ellie looked around the patio. The small iron fence, the beautiful stone floor, and the door in the side of the pizzeria were all brand new. The construction work had started last week, when the spring thaw came early. She loved how the project was turning out. In just a few more days, the outdoor patio would be ready to open. Weather permitting, she might be able to start seating people outside as early as Friday. It was just another step in her dream of turning the pizzeria into a real, family friendly sit-down restaurant. That didn't mean they would be stopping their pick-up and delivery services, of course.

Thinking of the new eat-in area made her remember what had been stressing her out so much over the past few days. There was no way around it; she would need to hire a new employee. She had already scheduled a few interviews, one of which was supposed to start in just a few minutes. It wasn't fair to her four employees to try to stretch them even further than they were already stretched. She knew that she should be excited at the prospect of a new face, but instead the idea just worried her. What if the person she hired turned out to be as bad as Xavier? The previous manager, before she had taken the role, had stolen thousands from her now-deceased grandfather and had almost driven the pizzeria into the ground.

"The lemonade is great. I'd ask for the recipe, but I'm guessing you won't give it up that easily."

Ellie shook herself and focused on the present. She smiled at Sam. "Family secret," she said. "But you're welcome to come and buy a glass whenever you'd like."

"I'll have to bring my kids out to eat here when the patio is finished. And you said you're going to let people bring dogs?"

"Yep. They can't come into the restaurant, but well-behaved dogs will be welcome on the patio."

"My kids will love that — we can bring our beagle, Casey."

"She's very welcome. We're going to have a supply of healthy dog cookies from the bakery in town, so your pup will have something to eat, too."

After gathering up the empty glasses, Ellie went back inside, almost running into Jacob, her delivery driver, as she pushed through the door. He jumped back, and she had to put a hand out to steady herself.

"We're going to need to do something about that," she said.

"I'm sorry, Ms. P.," he said. "I should have been more careful."

"Oh, it's not your fault, Jacob. I almost ran into Rose the other day. I should have thought to install two doors — one for in and one for out. With customers and employees trying to get through the same door, accidents are bound to happen. I'll print out a sign warning people to be careful and open the door slowly. Anyway, were you looking for me?"

"Yes, I was. Clara said she thought she'd seen you come out here. I wanted to talk to you about something kind of important."

Ellie frowned. Was Jacob about to quit? She hoped not. He had been working at the pizzeria for longer than she had been there. He was a great employee, and knew all of their regulars by name. He knew the town well enough that he could probably deliver pizzas with his eyes closed.

"Come into the kitchen with me. I'll drop this tray off and then we can step out back for a moment and chat."

The employee entrance opened into the parking lot at the rear of the building. It wasn't the most scenic place to talk, but it was the only place where they could get a semblance of privacy.

"So, what's going on?" she asked him.

"I've just been thinking about work. I love doing deliveries, but with the new outdoor eating area I know you're going to need more people working in the kitchen and working as servers. I probably should have brought this up sooner, but I'd love to start working in the restaurant more."

Thank goodness, he isn't quitting, she thought. "I'm sure we can make that work. Do you mind if I ask what changed? Have people not been tipping well?"

She knew that the tip money paid for most of her driver's gas and other driving expenses. It was important to her that her employees were being treated fairly, and she was determined to stand by them even if it meant losing a customer or two.

"Oh, no, the tipping has been fine. It's just getting to be kind of a lot, you know? Paying for gas and everything. I'm thinking of getting a new car, and I don't really want to run it into the ground like the one I have now. Plus, I actually really like working in the kitchen."

"Of course. Thanks for coming to me, Jacob. Can you keep working delivery until we get someone else hired? I'll ask you to train them, too, but after that we'll switch you to a different shift."

"Sounds good. Thanks, Ms. P.."

"Hey, there you are," Clara said, opening the employee exit and looking out at them. "I was looking for you, Ms. Pacelli. Some guy named Billy is here for an interview."

"Perfect timing, Clara," she said. "Take him to a booth and bring him a glass of lemonade. I'll join him in a second."

I really need an office, she thought as she went back inside. *Maybe that will be my next project.* The thought was tempting, but she would have to think about it more later. Right now, she had to focus on hiring a new delivery driver. Someone trustworthy, willing to work, and with a good car. It couldn't be too hard to find someone like that... could it?

PATTI BENNING

CHAPTER TWO

The Pacelli house was old and big, which meant there were a lot of small nooks and crannies that needed constant dusting and sweeping. Ellie lived with her grandmother, and though the eighty-five-year-old woman was determined to be as active as possible, she could no longer go up and down the stairs with ease, and tending the lawn was out of the question. That left Ellie with enough housework for two people, on top of her daily responsibilities at the pizzeria.

"You know, it would be nice to have a weekend where I don't have a single thing I have to do," she said to her little black and white papillon, Bunny. She was kneeling on the floor, scrubbing at a spot on the rug where someone had spilled a drink. The dog was watching her, her brown eyes following the rag as it rubbed back and forth.

"I know I could just put this off, but if I don't do it, no one will," Ellie continued. "It's not like I can relax while there's work to be done." It felt good to vent to the dog, even if Bunny couldn't understand her.

"Of course, I'd never tell Nonna how overwhelmed I feel sometimes. She does so much as it is." She gasped and glanced at her watch. The mention of her grandmother had reminded her that she was supposed to pick the woman up from physical therapy at two — and she was already late.

"Shoot. I'll have to finish this later. Come on, Bunny, you can ride along." She stood up and hurried to the foyer with the little dog at her heels. It didn't take her long to slip on her flats and clip the thin leather leash to her dog's collar. It was nice to be able to walk out of the house without putting on a coat first. Spring was in the air.

Ann Pacelli was waiting outside the physical therapist's office when Ellie pulled up. She had Bunny jump into the back seat, then got out to help the older woman into the passenger seat.

"Sorry I'm late, Nonna. I was busy cleaning, and it just slipped my mind. I've been trying to get everything done so I can have at least a few hours to relax before making dinner."

"Oh, it's alright, dear. It's so nice outside that I hardly noticed. And you know, you don't have to finish everything on your list today. It can wait. Or maybe I can do some of it —"

"I wouldn't ask you to do that," Ellie said. "You should be taking it easy. The last thing you need is to have another fall. You got lucky last time; you just broke your arm. It could have been a lot worse. At your age, a broken hip is a real concern."

"I know, I know. I just spent an hour with a doctor telling me the same thing. At least you don't make me do gymnastics in the pools while you tell me to take it easy."

She gave her grandmother an understanding smile. "I know it's hard. But we tell you to be careful about what you do because we want you around for a good long while. Personally, I would love to have someone tell me that I need to have someone else take over the housework. I'd get to sit around with a book and a cup of tea all day."

It was hard to imagine not being busy. She had been working forty or more hours every week since she had gotten out of graduate school, with hardly a vacation. She knew it was probably bad to be so addicted to a busy life, but she honestly couldn't imagine what it would be like to live a life without work to occupy her. She liked her job, which helped, but sometimes the never-ending list of things she had to do just got to her. Today, she still had to finish scrubbing the carpet, then Bunny needed a bath, and she should probably clean Marlowe's cage because the bird had thrown pieces of fruit out of her bowl that morning and —

"Ellie, watch out!"

She slammed on the brakes and swerved, narrowly missing the car that had come to a stop in front of her. Her eyes wide, she looked back at it in the rear-view mirror. What had she been thinking? She had always been a careful driver, but she hadn't even seen the car.

"Are you alright, Nonna? Bunny?" She made sure her two passengers were none the worse for the wear, then breathed a sigh of relief and tried to slow her racing heart down to a more normal pace. "I'm so sorry, you two. I was just planning out everything else I had to do today, and I guess I wasn't paying attention to the road."

"We're fine," Nonna assured her. "I don't think Bunny even realizes that something almost happened. But Ellie, I think you need to take some time off. Or at least take an evening to yourself. It's not good to work so much that you don't leave time for other things."

"Now would be the worst possible time to cut back on work. The patio's about to open, and we're hiring a new employee. He'll be in for training on Monday, and it will probably be a couple of weeks before he can work on his own."

"You've got to take care of yourself, sweetie." Her grandmother gave her a sly smile. "I just spent an hour listening to a doctor tell me the same thing, so I know I'm right about this. Promise me you'll take some time for yourself?"

Ellie reluctantly agreed. *What she doesn't realize is taking time to relax just means I'll have to do more work on another day,* she thought. *I'd really rather just get what needs to be done, done, and worry about everything else later.* A promise was a promise, though, and she resolved to set aside some time for rest and relaxation… after the new employee was trained up and ready to go.

CHAPTER THREE

"Clara, can you take Billy to the storage room and get him a hat and a shirt?" Ellie asked. "Then send him back to the kitchen and I'll start showing him around. You two met at his interview, right?"

"Sure did, Ms. P.. Come on, Billy. The storage room is this way. It's mostly just mops and buckets, nothing super interesting, but all stuff you'll need to know."

She bit her lip as Billy followed Clara down the hall. She hoped again that she had made the right choice. She had interviewed quite a few young men and women the week before, but Billy was the one she had the best feeling about. The tall, brown haired young man was around the same age as her other employees. She liked him because he seemed confident and intelligent, and was easy to talk to. She felt bad turning down some of the shyer interviewees, but answering the phone and building a rapport with the customers was an important part of the job.

Her promise to her grandmother was still on her mind, but she didn't see how she could take any extra time off with so much going on at the pizzeria. The outdoor eating area was complete, and was ready to open — though she was going to wait for a less windy day to officially cut the tape. Billy was promising, but he still needed to be trained, which would take up more of everyone's time. And of course, with the nicer weather, more and more people were showing up at the pizzeria during their busiest hours. In just a few months, it would be summer and the height of tourist season. The little Maine town would really come to life, and the pizzeria would be bustling with customers every night. If they weren't ready for the busy season, they would lose out on a lot of business.

Ellie headed towards the kitchen, glancing out the front window on her way. The clouds were racing across the sky, and she could hear the wind as it tore across the face of the building. She did not envy the people who worked at the electric company; she was sure they would be getting a lot of calls about downed power lines and outages today. Something loud rattled outside, and she winced.

Hopefully, the wind would die down soon, before doing any damage to the pizzeria — or worse, her house.

A few minutes later, Billy reappeared, wearing a black hat and a red shirt, both boasting the Papa Pacelli's name. He was grinning and tipped the hat proudly when he saw her.

"Gotta say, this place has great colors. Thanks again for hiring me. I'm looking forward to learning the job."

"It's not too difficult, once you get the hang of it. You'll be doing mostly deliveries, but everyone here also knows how to work the register and make pizzas. We'll start in here right now, but Clara will tell us if someone comes in to make an order so you can get some register practice, too. The most important thing is learning how to make new dough to replace what you use. Our number one rule is to replace any dough that you use. It takes a few hours to chill, so we definitely don't want to risk running out."

"Dough's important," he said. "Got it."

An hour later they had finished with the dough and moved on to where all of the various ingredients were kept. She was in the middle of telling him what to do if they were low on a certain ingredient, when her phone buzzed in her pocket. She glanced at it to see the call was from Russell.

"Let's take a break," she told her new employee. "You can make yourself a personal pizza or a calzone for lunch. Let's meet back here in twenty minutes. I'll let Clara take her break when you're finished."

She slid her finger across the screen to answer the call and stepped out through the employee entrance. It was rare, but not unheard of, for Russell to call her when he knew she was at work. It was near the time that she normally took a lunch break anyway; it was possible he was calling to see if he could stop in so they might split something.

"Hey," she said. "How are you?"

"Good," he said. She was relieved to hear that his voice was normal. She hated it, but whenever he called, she couldn't help but worry that he was the bearer of bad news. It was just one of the many things that came along with dating the sheriff of Kittiport. "How's everything there? I hope I didn't interrupt anything."

"I just told Billy, that's the new employee, to take a break. I'm glad you called, actually; otherwise, I might have worked right through lunch."

He chuckled. "Poor kid doesn't know what he's getting himself into. Actually, that's why I called."

"Billy?"

"No, you. You deserve a night off, and —"

"Wait, Russell… have you been talking to my grandmother?"

"She may have called me earlier today. But I've been wanting to take you out to dinner anyway, you know that."

EXOTIC PIZZA MURDER: BOOK NINE IN PAPA PACELLI'S PIZZERIA SERIES

She sighed. It was true. He kept trying to make plans with her, but she had been so busy making sure everything was going smoothly with the installation of the new patio that she kept putting it off. There had been one night that they had made plans, but he had been forced to go and help with a major three car accident on the state highway just outside of town. It seemed like it was hard to make plans, but even harder to keep them.

"I've got to be here every evening this week," she said. "Billy needs training, and Rose is out of town for spring break. We're going to be busier than ever with the patio opening. They need me."

"I'm sure your employees can handle it themselves for one night," he said gently. "Just last week you told me how well everything was going, and that they hardly needed you."

"But that was before I hired Billy…"

"Having Billy there should make things easier," he pointed out. "He can go on deliveries on his own once Jacob shows him the ropes, can't he? Kittiport isn't exactly a big town; it's not like he's going to get lost."

"But what if his car breaks down? Or what if the power goes out, or one of the ovens stops working…"

"Ellie, we're just going to be at the White Pine Kitchen. You'll have your phone with you. If something happens, you'll only be a few minutes away. So how about it? Dinner and a movie, and maybe a walk at the pier afterward, if it's nice out."

She took a deep breath and let it out slowly. She knew that she had to make time for other aspects of her life than work, and this would fulfill her promise to her grandmother as well as her obligations to Russell.

"Alright," she said. "Dinner it is. How about Thursday night? By then Billy should be trained enough that he won't need constant help, and we'll have worked out the kinks after opening up the patio."

"Thursday is perfect," he said. "I'll pick you up at five."

PATTI BENNING

CHAPTER FOUR

E llie spun in front of the mirror, trying to view herself from all angles. She was wearing a maroon dress with a gorgeous gold bracelet of her grandmother's and low black heels — she hadn't wanted to go too high in case they ended up taking that walk — and to tie it all off she had her favorite purse ready to go. She had left work a couple of hours ago, and had done her best not to check her phone constantly. The pizzeria hadn't been that busy when she had taken her leave, but it was getting to be dinner time, and that was sure to change soon. Billy and Jacob would be doing deliveries together unless something came up, and Clara and Iris would be handling the register and kitchen.

She was happy with Billy's progress. He was a quick learner, and got along well with her other employees. He got along with everyone, really. The customers all seemed to love him, and he had already learned many of the regulars by name. He was fitting in so well that she felt more comfortable with the thought of hiring even more employees in the future. *It might be a good idea to get some seasonal help for summer*, she thought. *It would be nice to take some of the work load off of my employees so they can enjoy their break from classes.*

She heard a knock downstairs and realized that Russell must be there. She gave herself one last look in the mirror, then grabbed her purse and went to greet him. In spite of all of her worries, she was really looking forward to tonight. It had been a while since she and Russell had gotten the chance to go out and just spend time together without any pressing time constraints. She really could use the evening off; it would be good for her to let her hair down occasionally.

The White Pine Kitchen was the nicest restaurant in town. Ellie only ever went there on dates with Russell, or for special occasions like her friend Shannon's birthday. It had been a while since the last time she had had reason to go, and she was pleasantly surprised to find that they had redone their decor.

"It looks like everyone is getting ready for spring," Russell said, looking around at the fresh flowers on the tables and the new lighting on the balcony. "It would be nice to eat out there sometime."

"I agree, though we should choose a night that's less windy. I don't want my food to blow away."

"That happened to Liam earlier. He stopped at the bakery and got a bagel for lunch. He put the bag on the roof of his car to unlock to door, and when he looked up, it was blowing down the road."

Ellie laughed. "Poor guy. I hope he got another one."

"The lady at the counter saw it happen and gave him one for free."

"People in Kittiport are so nice. You know, the other day Jacob and Billy were out on a delivery, and the customer gave them a double tip just to welcome Billy to the team. I love living and working in such a tight knit town."

"It's nice most of the time," Russell agreed. "Of course, there are downsides, too. If you don't like someone, it's almost impossible to avoid them."

"There's someone you're trying to avoid?" Ellie asked, surprised.

"Not me." He sighed. "I'm just thinking of a couple of guys we've had repeat complaints about. These two are neighbors, their kids are on the same baseball team, their wives both work at the same store. They compete over everything, and then get into shouting matches when something doesn't go their way. The other day, we got called in on a domestic disturbance complaint because they got into an argument at the grocery store over who was going to buy the last steaks from the butcher."

"That sounds ridiculous," Ellie said. "They're grown men. The should be setting a good example. Their kids are going to grow up just like them."

"And my successor will be breaking up arguments between them," Russell said with a sigh. "It never ends. But enough about my job. How's the new patio working out for you?"

They paused to place their order. Ellie took a sip of her wine before answering his question.

"It's doing even better than I hoped, with it being so early in the year still. I almost wish I had thought to add the outdoor seating last year. The view of the marina is just perfect. I think we're going to be packed during tourist season."

"Good." He raised his glass in a toast. "To the pizzeria."

She smiled and clinked her glass against hers. "To the pizzeria — and the rest of this crazy town."

Her phone buzzed just as she lifted the glass to her lips. She pulled it out of her purse and checked the screen. It was a text message from Jacob. She shot a guilty glance at Russell.

"Sorry," she said. "It's from work. I should probably at least read it. I don't think Jacob would interrupt us unless it was important."

"Go ahead. You know my work phone is always on, too. I can't exactly blame you for answering yours. How many times have we had to cancel plans because the department needed me?"

"Yeah, but you're the sheriff. You save lives." She wrinkled her nose. "I just make pizzas. This won't take long, I promise."

She opened the message and frowned at what she saw. *Sorry, I had to leave early. Got sick. Clara, Iris, and Billy said they can handle everything.*

"What is it?"

"Jacob is sick and left early." She was glad he had gone home; she had a strict policy about people not coming in if they were ill. Even with frequent hand washing, it just wasn't sanitary to have germs around food. She just wished it could have happened on a different night. Was Billy ready to handle the deliveries on his own? "Do you think they'll be okay without me? It's dinner time, and the pizzeria will be at its busiest."

The sheriff covered her hand with his. "Ellie, they'll be fine. Go if you want to, but I'd really rather you stay here and finish dinner with me. We don't get time together like this very often."

"I know." She took a deep breath, then smiled at him. "You're right. They'll be fine. I need to stop worrying so much."

An hour later, Ellie smiled up at the waitress as the woman delivered her favorite dessert; lava cake with real vanilla ice cream. She was glad that she had let her grandmother and then Russell talk her into taking some time off to just relax. She had forgotten how much she enjoyed just being with Russell. *I really need to make more time for him,* she thought. *And for Shannon, too. I don't want to be so busy with the pizzeria that I lose my friends.* She realized with a rush of guilt how many times she had turned down an invitation from Shannon to get together in just the past few weeks. She had been ignoring her very best friend.

I'll be able to take some more time off once Billy is fully trained, she rationalized. *It's just that these past few weeks have been crazy, with all of the construction for the patio going on.* Things would get back to normal soon, and she was sure once they did, she would stop feeling so overworked.

"What movie do you want to see?" Russell asked her as he started on his slice of New York style cheesecake. "There are two playing at the Kittiport Theater, and both of them start in the next hour."

He slid his phone across the table so she could read the movie descriptions. Both of them looked interesting to her. It had been a while since she had seen anything in the theater.

"I'd be happy with either one. Which do you want to see more?"

He was about to answer when his phone rang. "See, it's not just you," he said as he answered it.

Smiling, she poked her spoon into the lava cake. She was glad that they both had jobs that demanded a lot of attention. She was sure it made them more understanding toward each other when work got in the way of time together.

She glanced up, and was surprised to see Russell's brows drawn together in consternation. *Something bad must have happened*, she thought. *Something really bad.*

"Right, I'll meet you there in a few minutes, Liam. I've got to pay for dinner first. Get his wife and kid out of the house. Find some place to set them up for the night. I'll question them when I get done at the house." He hung up and turned a grim look to Ellie.

"What happened?" she asked, feeling her face go pale.

"A murder," he said. "I'm sorry, but we've got to go. I'll drop you off at home first. Can we take a raincheck on that movie?"

"Of course," she said. "It sounded like the victim had a wife and a child? They need you right now, that's more important than any movie."

He gave her a quick kiss, then called for the check. Ellie felt terrible; someone had died, and had left behind a family. She was sure tonight wouldn't be easy for Russell. She couldn't even imagine trying to talk to the dead man's grieving wife. *I don't know how he*

42

does his job, she thought. *Even if he catches the killer, there won't be any happy ending for the victim's family. Their lives are changed forever, and nothing will ever put things back to normal.*

CHAPTER FIVE

It was still early when Ellie got home. Normally she would be at the pizzeria for another hour, at least. She knew that she should learn to let go, but Jacob's text had made her anxious. What if her three employees got overwhelmed? Normally three people would be enough to manage Papa Pacelli's even on the busiest of nights, but Billy was still new and needed help occasionally. There needed to be one person in the kitchen while there was food in the oven, which meant that they would have to plan their bathroom breaks carefully.

They're probably fine, she thought. *Thursday nights are busy, but they aren't that much busier than the rest of the week. Clara's been working there for ages. She knows how to handle things.* Despite her assurances to herself, she just couldn't relax. It seemed ridiculous for her to sit at home while Russell was out in town dealing with the aftermath of a brutal crime, and her employees were as busy as bees trying to keep things going smoothly at the pizzeria.

"I'm going in," she said aloud, shooting a glance toward the kitchen where her grandmother was relaxing with her normal cup of tea. She knew the older woman would want her to stay home and let the others do their job, but she couldn't ignore the fact that the pizzeria was her responsibility. She could take another, less busy evening off. Tonight, Papa Pacelli's needed her.

The parking lot was more than halfway full when she pulled in twenty minutes later. She had only ever seen it more full once; the evening of the local high school's homecoming game. The combination of the nice weather, the fact that many schools were out on spring break, and the new outdoor eating area must have made Papa Pacelli's the place to go that evening. The breeze had died down, and she saw that most of the outdoor tables were full. People were laughing and eating, and she even saw a few dogs lying politely under the chairs. Smiling, Ellie let herself in through the employee entrance.

"Oh, Ms. P., you surprised me," Iris said. She gave a small laugh. "I was expecting Billy."

"I just thought I'd stop in and see how things were going. Is he out on a delivery?"

"Yeah. This is his third one on his own."

"How has he been doing?"

"He was a bit late after the first one, but other than that he's been great. He hasn't lived here his whole life like some of us, so he probably just got turned around."

Ellie chuckled. "I know the feeling." She had grown up in the small northern Maine town, but she and her mother had moved away before she graduated high school. She didn't know the town as well as someone like Russell or Shannon, who had lived there their entire lives, did. "How has the evening been going other than that? I heard Jacob got sick and had to go home."

"Yeah. He felt really bad. He thinks it was food poisoning from some fast food he got earlier. It probably wasn't contagious, but he knows how you are about us going home if we're sick."

"I'm glad he decided to be safe about it." She had worked hard to build up the pizzeria's reputation. The last thing she needed was for people to get sick from one of her employees. In such a small town, accusations like that would spread like wildfire.

"Everything else has been fine. People are happy. The wait time is about twenty minutes for a pizza, and no one's complaining. The patio is super popular. People love that they can bring their dogs. Clara and I have been switching off serving tables and working in the kitchen."

"It sounds like you got that handled," Ellie said. "I should have known you would take care of it."

The employee door opened behind her and she moved out of the way as Billy came in. He raised his eyebrows when he saw her.

"Hi, Ms. Pacelli. I thought you were on a date tonight."

Iris shot him a look, but Ellie just chuckled. "I was. The problem with dating a sheriff, is that sometimes things come up that are just more important than dinner. We had a nice meal, we'll just have to catch the movie later."

"I saw a bunch of police cars while I was heading back from a delivery. I wonder if that was related to what happened?"

"It could be. He got the call almost an hour after Jacob left, so you would have been doing deliveries on your own."

"I hope whatever happened wasn't too serious," Iris said. "And I hope it wasn't anyone we know."

Ellie remained silent. She didn't know if Russell wanted it getting out yet that there had been a murder. Sometimes she wished he wouldn't tell her these things until the general public knew about them — but of course, if he didn't tell her she knew she would probably be just as frustrated. Tomorrow, when he called her, she would learn more. Until then, she would have to keep her employees in the dark.

CHAPTER SIX

"Oh no, Russell., not another one."

Ellie sat down on her bed, feeling all the energy go out of her. This marked the second death in a week. Things had just started to quiet down after news about the first murder got out.

"Is it related to the first one at all?"

"It's hard to say. This guy had no connection that we can see to Andy Worth, and the method in which he was killed was different, but it was the same sort of situation. He answered the door, and someone attacked him. This person's wife was at work, but he also lived with his brother, who came down a moment after he was killed and saw the killer drive off."

She had been shocked and dismayed to learn that the first victim had been one of the very men Russell had spoken of at the beginning of their date, the guy who was in constant competition with his neighbor. She hadn't known the man at all, but even just the knowledge that they had talked about him only minutes or hours before he was killed chilled her to the core. How could a life be taken so quickly, so easily?

"What's going on in this town?" she asked. "This is insane. I don't even feel safe at my grandmother's anymore."

"Just don't answer the door for anyone you don't know. You have my number, and the sheriff's department's number, right? If someone you don't recognize shows up, just call me right away, even if they aren't acting suspicious."

"I will," she promised. "I just hope my grandmother remembers not to answer the door either. I'll leave a note to remind her."

"I'm sure the two of you will be fine. These two men probably had a connection that we're just missing."

"I hope so. It's horrible enough that people are dying, but if it's random, it's even more frightening." Something occurred to her. "Wait, you said the last victim's brother saw the killer drive away. Does that mean he saw the license plate?"

Russell sighed. "Sadly, no. He just saw the tail lights. He said he thinks they belonged to a car, as opposed to an SUV or a truck, but he was understandably distracted by his brother."

"Of course. That must have been so horrible."

"I'm going to find the person or people who are doing this," the sheriff said, his voice determined. "It will help the victim's families to know the killer is facing justice, though of course nothing will bring their loved ones back."

Ellie realized that these cases must be hitting him close to home. His wife had been killed years ago, and he had never found the person responsible for her death. She didn't know much about what had happened; he never talked about it, and she didn't ask about it. She figured he didn't want to relive the past — she knew she wouldn't.

"I know you'll solve these cases," she told him. "You're the best sheriff I know."

To her relief, he chuckled. "And how many do you know?"

"Well, one. But even if I knew a hundred, you'd be the best."

"I'm glad you have confidence in my crime solving abilities. I hope you're right. I hope we catch this killer, before he strikes again."

Ellie and Russell said their goodbyes and got off the phone. It was early evening, and she was working in the kitchen at the pizzeria, trying to stay on top of things. Billy was out on a delivery, and Jacob was enjoying his first full shift as a server. She checked the orders and realized with relief that she was all caught up. *Now to make some dough, and start tackling those dishes,* she thought. *I should top off the lemonade, too.*

She had just finished making the third dough ball to put in the fridge when the employee door swung open and Billy came into the kitchen. He waved at her, then sat down at the kitchen table.

"Can I take my dinner break now, Ms. P.? I'm starved. Probably shouldn't have skipped lunch."

"Go ahead, Billy. We have one more delivery to go out, but I'll ask Jacob if he'll do it. He said he wouldn't mind doing them once in a while. You've been working hard, you deserve it."

"Thanks. I'll make more lemonade while I'm at it. That stuff is good."

She smiled. So far, Billy had been a wonderful addition to the team. He never complained when she asked him to do something. He still seemed to have some trouble finding some of the addresses, but she couldn't blame him. Cell phone service was spotty at best in Kittiport, so using GPS wasn't very reliable. The best part was, he was happy to work as many hours as he could get. She was so glad that she had made the jump to hire another employee; it gave them all a lot more freedom and flexibility in scheduling.

While Billy put his personal pizza together, she went out into the main room to find Jacob, who was just coming in from the patio with an armful of dirty dishes. "I can take those," she said. "Would you mind doing a delivery really quick while Billy's on his lunch break? I put the pizza box in the bag already."

"Yeah, no problem. Where's the car sign?"

Recently, she had ordered a new magnetic sign that her employees could put on top of their cars while they were doing deliveries. She liked that it made them look more professional, plus she had a feeling that it also made other drivers more forgiving when her employees were driving slowly and trying to find addresses in the dark.

"Probably still on Billy's car. When you get back, do you want to take your break? I can put a pizza in for you while you're gone."

"Sure, thanks, Ms. P.."

"Pineapple and pepperoni?"

"You got it."

She pushed through the swinging door into the kitchen and dropped the dishes off in the sink while Jacob got his keys and the bag with the pizza in it. As he left, she went back out to the main eating area to see if any of her customers needed anything. Her work as manager never ended, but she didn't mind much at all.

PATTI BENNING

CHAPTER SEVEN

"Can I get you another lemonade?" she asked, approaching a table where a small family of three was seated. "And another soda?"

"Yeah," the kid said.

"Brian, what do you say?"

"Ugh. I mean yes, please," he said, rolling his eyes at his mother.

"I'll take another lemonade, too, thanks," said the man.

"Coming right up."

As she was coming back with the drinks on a tray, she couldn't help but overhear a part of their conversation. "I keep expecting to see Andy walk through those doors with Devon and Maria in tow like they did every Wednesday night. It's hard to believe I'll never see him again."

"Oh, Jason, I can't believe it either," said the woman, who Ellie assumed was his wife. "Poor Maria, I can't even imagine… and poor Devon, growing up without a father."

"I thought you didn't like him, Dad?" asked the kid.

"We had a friendly rivalry, that's all," said the father, ruffling the kid's hair. "You'll understand one day. Now look, here comes the nice lady with the drinks. What do you say, Brian?"

"Thanks!"

Ellie chuckled as she put the drinks down on the table. "You enjoy yourselves, now. If you need anything else, don't hesitate to flag anyone wearing a Papa Pacelli's shirt down."

As she pushed through the patio door to check on the outside guests, she mulled over the conversation she had heard. Those people had known Andy, the first victim, the one that had died the week before. The seemed like such a normal family; it was a frightening reminder that anyone could be the victim of a crime. *Sometimes I forget what a small town this is*, she thought. *These murder victims are more than just names or an interesting conversation topic. They are actual people, whose deaths effect everyone.*

She was still feeling down a few minutes later, when she was back in the kitchen and scrubbing the dishes. Another murder in her beloved town... how much more of this could they take? What if someone else was killed before Russell caught the perpetrator? She didn't know if he would ever be able to forgive himself, even though it wouldn't be his fault, of course.

The employee door opened. Ellie glanced up to see Jacob come in. She gave him a nod, then turned back to the sink. She was surprised when he came up beside her and spoke to her in a low voice.

"Ms. P., where's Billy?"

"He's taking a pizza out to someone on the patio. Why?"

"I found something in his car, and I think you should see it."

Ellie blinked. "In his car? Why were you in his car?"

"Because he had the magnetic sign in the back seat. I had to get it for the delivery. Anyway —"

"Why was the sign *in* the car?"

"I don't know, but that's not the point. Would you just come out and look at this?"

She was surprised. Usually Jacob was the most relaxed of her employees, but right now he sounded more agitated than she had ever heard him.

"Okay, I'll go look at whatever it is you want me to see."

She rinsed and dried her hands off, then followed him outside. He made a beeline for Billy's car, a nice sedan that was just a few years old. With a furtive look back at the restaurant, he opened the back door and gestured his boss over. Feeling guilty — no matter how she looked at it, this was a gross invasion of Billy's privacy — she approached.

"What am I supposed to be looking at?" she asked.

"Look in his bag. I didn't touch it at all, I swear. It was open when I got into his car to get the sign."

Ellie peered at the backpack on the floor of the back seat and gasped when she saw the tightly bundled wads of cash poking out of it. *That's a lot of money*, she thought. *I pay fair wages, but I don't pay my employees* that *much.* There was also a wallet. Carefully, she took it out and looked at the ID. It most definitely did not belong to Billy. She thought she recognized the man in the picture — one of their regulars.

64

"Where did he get it all?" she asked Jacob in a hushed voice.

"I don't know, but he can't be getting it legally, can he? I mean, who carries around that much cash in their car, and doesn't even lock their doors?"

"We can't just assume he's done something illegal to get it. That wouldn't be fair. Maybe he just doesn't trust banks. Or maybe…" she sighed. "I don't know."

"Nothing's been off with the pizzeria?" he asked.

"What do you mean?"

"The, ah, finances."

She frowned. "You mean, you think he might have been stealing from us? That's a very serious accusation to make. Besides, I'm sure I would have noticed if that much money had gone missing."

She stared at the bills poking out of his bag for a second longer. There *were* a lot of ones and fives in there. She shook her head. She couldn't jump to conclusions. It wasn't illegal to carry around large amounts of cash. Billy hadn't given her a reason not to trust him; until he did, she would treat him just like any of her other employees.

PATTI BENNING

CHAPTER EIGHT

E llie dropped a pair of sugar cubes into her teacup, then propped the tray against her hip and carried it out of the kitchen and into the living room where Shannon was waiting. Her friend sat on the couch with Bunny curled up contentedly next to her. Marlowe was on the back of the armchair across the room, her head tucked under one wing, snoozing.

"I've got tea and the last of the blueberry muffins Nonna made this morning," Ellie said. "I figure we can make a salad for lunch in a little bit. We've got plenty of fresh ingredients."

"That sounds great," Shannon said. "This is so nice. We haven't spent the day together, just us girls, in I don't know how long."

"It's my fault, I've been insanely busy. Now that the construction is finished and Billy's pretty much trained, things have calmed down a lot." She faltered slightly at the mention of her employee's name. Ever since Jacob had discovered the cash in his car, she had kept a close eye on him. Sometimes she thought she caught him sliding something into his pocket after serving tables, but she hadn't noticed any money go missing, and none of her other employees had complained about missing tips. Part of her wanted to just confront him about it, but then she would have to admit that she and Jacob had gone into his car without his knowledge, and she knew that they had both been wrong to do that.

"Well, good. I've missed my best friend. I love James, but sometimes I just need someone else to talk to, you know?"

"I completely understand," Ellie said, taking the seat on the other side of Bunny, who was eying the muffins on the tray. "It will be good to catch up. Has Russell told you about the cases he's working on?"

"Yeah, he stopped by the other morning to borrow some tools from James, and he told us all about the murders. I heard about both deaths on the news, but hearing about it from him made it seem so much more real. James is all worried about me being home alone. I told him I'm not about to go opening the door to strangers when people have been dying."

"Russell was worried about me too. It *is* scary. I haven't had a chance to talk to him much for a few days. Do you know if he's had any leads on the case?"

"I think he told James that he was looking into one of the guy's neighbors, but he didn't make it sound too promising."

I wonder if he was talking about Jason, the guy that Andy had that rivalry with, she wondered. She could see how on the surface, he seemed like the perfect suspect, but after overhearing his conversation with his family at the pizzeria, she didn't think he was the one who had done it.

"He said that both victims' wives worked at the same place, so that could be another lead," her friend continued. "It feels like he's reaching with that, though."

"I don't see why someone would kill two men, just because of where their wives work. Of course, I don't understand what could motivate someone to kill in the first place." She gave a shudder. "I'm glad that there are people like Russell in the world who track the bad guys down."

"Yeah, Russ is pretty cool. James thinks he works too much, though. Before the two of you started dating, he was even more obsessed with his job. Other than our weekly dinners, I don't think he ever took an evening off. At least now he makes time for other things."

"We're both workaholics," Ellie said with a smile, stirring her tea. "I wouldn't have it any other way. I am glad my job isn't that stressful, though. I think I would go crazy if I had to do his. Having so many people rely on me, not just for food, but for their lives…" She shook her head.

"It's just been a bad year. Before you moved here last summer, it had been almost three years since there had been a suspicious death. The worst things they had to deal with were car accidents and the occasional break in, and of course damage from the winter storms."

"Still, I don't know how he does it. He had to go and talk to the wives of the murder victims, to question them right after their husbands were found. I would be a mess if I had to do that. As it is, I can't stop thinking about the poor women."

They both fell silent for a few moments, before Shannon cleared her throat and changed the subject. "Enough about that. Let's talk about something less depressing. I've had to think about these cases all day at work; I need a break from it."

Shannon worked as a reporter for the local newspaper. She usually wrote a column about local events, from the annual Lobster Fest, to announcements from the knitting club, but recently had been chosen to write some of the front-page stories as well. Ellie loved that her friend was getting an opportunity to write more. She enjoyed seeing her friend's name on the front page, and knew that James was proud of his wife, too.

Casting around for something else to discuss, she thought once again about Billy. "There is something odd going on with my new employee," she began.

PATTI BENNING

When she told her friend about the money that Jacob had found poking out of Billy's backpack, Shannon frowned.

"Have you told Russell about this?"

"No. Then I'd have to admit to him that I snooped in Billy's car, which I'm embarrassed to do. I also feel like he has enough on his plate without worrying about one of my employees. I hired the guy, it's my responsibility to make sure that he's not doing something shady under the table."

"You know Russ would want you to tell him."

Ellie sighed. "I know. But I don't want to distract from the murders. People's lives are more important than this. If Billy is stealing from me, I can handle it on my own. I don't need Russell to do *everything* for me."

Her friend chuckled. "I guess you have a point. What's the plan, then? How are you going to catch this guy in the act?"

"Honestly, I don't even know what act I'm trying to catch him in. That was a lot of money. I would have noticed if that much was missing from the pizzeria's accounts. I don't know if he's been gambling, stealing from customers, or what. Like I told Jacob, he might not even be doing anything wrong. There are valid reasons for someone to carry around that much cash."

"Like what?"

"Well, I can't think of any, but I'm sure they exist."

Her friend burst out laughing, and a moment later, Ellie joined her. It felt good to talk with Shannon. Spending time with her best friend always seemed to make her feel better, no matter what crazy stuff was going on in her life at the time.

PATTI BENNING

CHAPTER NINE

"I don't know about this," Ellie said. "If he figures out what we're doing…"

"How will he?" Iris asked. "At least this way we'll know for sure if he's been stealing. If we just ask him, he'll feel like we don't trust him."

"We don't trust him," Jacob pointed out.

Ellie sighed. Things had been going so well, until the drawer had come up short of money two nights in a row. Billy had been working both nights, and while she had no proof he had taken the money, to say she was suspicious would be an understatement. She hated going behind his back, but if he *wasn't* doing anything illegal, making an accusation to his face might be even worse.

"Look," she said. "We're only going to try this once. We'll leave the money out. If he takes it, we'll confront him. If he leaves it, we'll let it drop, okay?"

Her employees nodded. She wished that Iris hadn't overheard her and Jacob talking about the money they had found in Billy's car. It would be one thing if it was just between the two of them — Jacob had been the one to find the money, after all, and despite all of the anxiety the issue had caused her, she was glad he had told her. Bringing Iris into the matter felt too sneaky for her liking. Billy didn't need all of the employees talking about him behind his back. She wanted the pizzeria to be a safe place for all of them, not a place where they had secrets from each other.

Billy was currently on a delivery. When he got back, Ellie would ask him to take a shift at the register while she handled the deliveries for a while — she wouldn't be lying if she said she would enjoy the chance to get out of the restaurant for a bit, and it was true that he still needed more practice ringing customers up. Before she left, she would leave a couple of bills on the counter by the register and tell him that a customer had overpaid. Iris and Jacob would be watching to see if he took the money, or left it where it was. It wasn't a complex plan, but it should at the very least tell her whether her new employee was honest or not.

"Ms. P., he's pulling in now," Jacob said, peering out the drive-up window in the kitchen.

"Alright, everyone, just act normal. Remember, we don't want to mislead him any more than we have to."

The first part of the plan went smoothly. Ellie placed a pair of twenties on the counter before sending Billy out to the register with instructions to give the money back if a customer came looking for it. Of course, she knew no one would come back looking for money since no one had actually overpaid, but she figured it was a good ruse. If the money was gone when she got back, then she would know that Billy was being dishonest.

It had been a long time since Ellie had been on delivery duty. She had forgotten how peaceful it could be to load up a few pizzas in the car and head out, away from the hustle and bustle of the restaurant. Kittiport was a pretty little town, and always a pleasure to drive through, even in the evening. The harbor with lights from the boats, and the smell of wood smoke filled the air as people began lighting their fire places. It was still early enough in the year that it got chilly in the evenings, so the sight of smoke plumes over houses wasn't at all uncommon. She left her windows down just a hair to allow the early spring scents of her home town into the car, turned on her favorite radio station, and pulled out of the parking lot towards her first delivery destination.

"Keep the change, dear," the elderly woman said, smiling at her. "You have a nice evening."

"You, too," Ellie said, returning the smile. "Thanks for choosing Papa Pacelli's."

She got back in her car, still smiling. It was always nice to see a familiar face unexpectedly. This first delivery had been to an old friend of her grandmother's, someone who Ellie saw occasionally when she dropped her nonna off at restaurants and get-togethers.

She truly loved how tightly knit the town was… and it made her all the angrier at the person or people that had committed the two murders. Kittiport should be the sort of town where people didn't bother to lock their doors, but lately it had been the kind of town where people were afraid to open them.

Her next delivery was a mile or two out of town in one of the nicer suburbs. She hadn't had much occasion to drive out that direction, so she pulled out her phone and turned on the GPS. She had only gone a few miles when a robotics voice told her that the GPS signal had been lost.

"Great," she muttered. "I've just got to remember that I'm looking for Rabbit Woods subdivision. It can't be that hard to find."

It took her longer than she would have liked to find the subdivision, then she drove around in circles for another few minutes before she found the correct drive. She triple checked the address on the receipt before pulling into the driveway of a sizable two-story house.

"Here we go," she said. "The last delivery before I can go back to the pizzeria and see if Billy took the money or not."

She grabbed the insulated bag that kept the pizza warm, hefted the two-liter of soda, and made her way up the walk to the porch. Her steps faltered when she saw that the door was already open. Was she supposed to let herself inside? Some people were casual about deliveries, but she didn't know anyone who would leave their front door wide open like that, especially on such a cool spring evening.

She took the last few steps up to the porch and raised her hand to knock on the door frame, but her hand never made contact with the wood. Her eyes focused on the dark form lying just inside the door. She hadn't seen the shape at first; she had been looking at eye level, expecting someone to walk up. There was no mistaking the dark red stain beneath the man lying sprawled in the entrance as anything other than blood.

Somehow managing to hold onto the pizza, Ellie took a stumbling step backwards and let out a scream.

CHAPTER TEN

T he lights from the police cars and ambulance looked out of place in the quiet little subdivision. Ellie shivered and rubbed her hands up and down her arms. The temperature had dropped even farther. She knew that she should probably be sitting inside her car, but she couldn't seem to tear her gaze away from the scene that was unfolding in front of her. A minivan had just pulled into the driveway, and she immediately recognized the dark-haired woman that got out of the front seat. Nancy, wife of Jason, the man that she had found dead.

Ellie was unable to look away as the woman approached the house slowly, her hand going up to her face in an expression of shock as she realized what she was looking at. She recognized Bethany's blond hair as the young deputy rushed to give what comfort she could to the woman. Her gaze flicked back to the van, and she saw a shadow move behind the darkened windows. She realized that the son must be in the back, waiting for his mother to figure out what was going on.

"Oh, my goodness," she muttered. It was too much for her. She fumbled for her car door and slid inside. She wished she could just go home, but she had promised Russell that she would talk to him as soon as he was done with the paramedics.

What's going on in this town? she wondered. *Three deaths so far, and unless the killer left some evidence behind this time, this probably isn't the end of it.* It was intriguing to her that this victim and the first victim had known each other. Was that a link between the crimes, or just a coincidence? In a town as small as Kittiport, it wasn't too unlikely of an occurrence.

A knock at the passenger window startled her. She looked up to see Russell peering in. She unlocked the door and gestured for him to join her.

"How are you?" he asked as he sat down in the passenger seat.

"Not great. Pretty bad, actually," she admitted. "But it could be worse." Her eyes were on the huddled form of Jason's wife. The poor woman's life had changed forever. Her world would never be the same again.

"This is the third one," the sheriff said. She turned to see him shaking his head sadly. "Three murders, three wives left behind, and two of them had kids. I haven't felt so drained by a case since…" He fell silent, then said, "Well, it's been a while."

"They were in my restaurant earlier this week," she said in a quiet voice. "I remember, because I overheard them talking about the first victim. If I knew then that they would only have a few more days left together, I would have told them to leave, to get out of town. I would have paid for a vacation for the three of them to the Bahamas if that's what it took to get them out and prevent this."

"There's no way you could have known," he told her.

"I know." She sighed.

"Do you want to give your statement now? If you'd rather wait —"

"No, no, now is okay. I want to get it over with. Plus, it's all still fresh in my mind."

"Alright. Let's begin with the call he put in to order the pizza…"

After Russell finished questioning her, Ellie was free to go. While every bone in her body ached to go back home and curl up in bed with a hot cup of tea while she tried not to cry herself to sleep, she knew that she couldn't just vanish from the pizzeria. She had to at least go back and tell her employees what had happened.

When she let herself in the employee entrance, she was surprised by Jacob's enthusiastic greeting. "Ms. P.! There you are. We were getting worried." He glanced quickly around the kitchen, then added in a lower voice, "Billy didn't touch the money. Iris and I made sure we left him alone with it for a while, but nothing happened. I don't think he's been doing anything wrong."

"That's good," she said, not quite paying attention. Her suspicions about her new employee seemed inconsequential now.

"Did something happen, Ms. P.?" he asked. "You were gone an awfully long time."

She told him about the murder, her voice shaking. She realized it was probably a good thing that she had decided to take the last two pizzas out for delivery, otherwise one of her employees might have been the one to find the corpse. Better her than them, she thought.

"Wow, I can't believe that someone else was killed," he replied when she was done. "Were there any witnesses? Did anyone see the killer drive away this time?"

"Not that I know of," she told him. "Russell was still questioning the neighbors when I left. I just stopped in to update you guys and drop off the insulated bag and the delivery sign before going home. I need some space to process everything."

"I'll let Iris and Billy know what happened," he said. "Go on home, Ms. P. We'll be fine here."

PATTI BENNING

CHAPTER ELEVEN

The *Eleanora* bobbed gently on the waves in the harbor. Ellie hoisted Bunny into her arms and stepped from the dock to the boat, glad it was a calm day. It had been a while since she had been out on the boat that her grandfather had named after her, and she was eager for the feeling of freedom that came when she was out on the open water.

"There you are," Russell said, coming along the dock. "I was wondering who made it here first."

"Here, let me help you," she said, reaching to take the cooler from him before he made the step over to the boat. "This is heavy. What all did you pack?"

"Anything and everything we could possibly want for a picnic," he said with a grin.

"If it weighed any more, I might be afraid the boat would sink," she joked. "You ready to go?"

"Yep. Untie her, and I'll get us out of the marina."

She undid the rope that tethered the boat to the dock and then took a seat as the sheriff began to maneuver the boat out of the maze that was the marina. She was happy to steer when they were on the open water, but didn't trust herself to do it around so many expensive vessels. With her luck, she would crash into some millionaire's boat and end up owing more than she would ever make in her life.

It was a warm day on shore, but as they got into the open ocean, she became glad that she had thought to bring a light jacket. There was a strong breeze, which would have made the trip miserable if she hadn't had something warm to put on. After one strong gust too many, Bunny gave her an annoyed look and got up to go into the cabin. Ellie laughed and followed her, pulling open one of the bench seats to withdraw the small, bright orange doggy life vest that she had bought a few weeks ago.

"I'd better put this on you," she told her dog. "We wouldn't want you getting lost if you fall overboard."

The vest served the double purpose of both life-saving equipment and a windbreaker, and after Ellie had strapped it on, the little papillon looked a lot happier. She had fallen into the ocean the year before, and while the dog hadn't seemed spooked by the experience, her owner sure had been. Bunny was so small that a shark could probably swallow her in a single gulp. Granted, Ellie had yet to see a shark off the Maine coast, but her dog's safety still concerned her.

"Where do you want to go?" Russell asked her. "The normal spot?"

"Sure. It's our favorite for a reason."

Their favorite spot was a stretch of coast that bordered the state park. The stark cliffs that towered above the ocean were lined with pine trees. It should have been a forbidding view, but Ellie had always found it beautiful. If they were lucky, they may even see some of the seabirds nesting in the cracks and crags on the side of the cliff.

It felt good to get out and away from town. She hadn't been able to shake the low mood that had taken over since she had found the body. She hardly even cared about the fact that the drawer had come up short another couple of times. Nothing seemed important after witnessing the woman's grief when she drove up to her husband's murder scene. Both Russell and she had decided that they needed at least a few hours in which the murders didn't touch their lives at all.

"It really is beautiful here," she said softly and Russell slowly guided the boat nearer to the cliffs. "I'm glad winter is over. Being outside is just good for the soul, and a whole lot more pleasant when I'm not freezing my face off."

The sheriff chuckled. "I don't mind the winter so much, as long as it doesn't storm more than once or twice. This past year was worse than usual. It's over now, at least. I'm sure I'll enjoy this spring weather more once I don't have these cases hanging over my head."

"We aren't out here to talk about that," she reminded him.

They had already beaten the subject to death, going over the same thing again and again wouldn't do anything but put them both in a bad mood. She knew that things were already tense at the sheriff's department. Everyone wanted to find the killer, or killers, but every lead they thought they had ended up being a dead end. The one link between all three men was that their wives all worked at the same store — but no matter who they questioned, they couldn't make sense of a motive. How could the wives working together be tied to the deaths of their husbands?

"You're right, you're right," he said, putting his hands up in mock defeat. "I think this is a good spot. I'll drop anchor, and we can unpack that picnic. I even packed a little something for Bunny, in the hopes that it would keep her from begging us for our food."

Ellie grinned. Her little dog had a big appetite. She was supposed to be on a diet, but it wasn't working out so well. She knew Nonna still slipped the papillon food under the table, and Marlowe seemed to enjoy tossing the food out of her dish and onto the floor, and then watching Bunny eat it. Ellie knew she was outnumbered when even the bird joined in on sneaking her dog treats.

The picnic that Russell had packed was delicious. They ate it out of the wind, on the small table in the cabin. Bunny chewed on her bone, occasionally glancing up at the two people as they ate their ham and cheese sandwiches. Ellie popped a grape into her mouth, feeling happier than she had in a long time. It was so peaceful out here on the water, it was easy to feel some of the stress of the past few days slipping away.

"How's the pizzeria doing? With everything that's been going on at the sheriff's department, we haven't really had a chance to talk about your work lately."

She bit her lip, struggling internally for a moment. She had often been tempted to bring up her suspicions about Billy, but didn't want to worry Russell. He was already dealing with enough, and he didn't need anything to distract him from the murders and cause him to possibly miss a clue. On the other hand, she knew he would want her to tell him. Besides, it would give them something to talk about besides the three dead men.

"Things have been alright," she said. "The patio was a success. James did such a great job on it. I told him he gets free pizzas for life. He didn't accept, though."

"He wouldn't," Russell said with a smile. "I'm sure he's glad you're happy with the work, though."

"We've been busier than ever. I can't wait for this summer when we start getting tourists."

"It's good you hired someone else. You're probably going to get overwhelmed as it is."

She sighed. It was time to tell him. Maybe he would be able to put her mind at ease.

"Actually, I'm not sure hiring Billy was a good idea." She went on to tell him about the money that Jacob had found in his car when he opened the vehicle to grab the delivery sign off the back seat. She also told him about the little test she and her employees had done the night of the murder. "He didn't seem interested in the money at all," she finished. "The thing is, the drawer has been off a few more times since. Nothing major, but it only seems to happen when he's working."

"Ellie, you should have told me this sooner. That sounds like a lot of money for someone to be carrying around. Does he know you know about it?"

"No. At least, I don't think so. Other than me, Jacob and Iris are the only ones who know. Jacob because he found it, obviously, and Iris just happened to overhear the two of us talking about it. I told them that if he didn't take the money we left on the counter, we would just drop the issue. They don't know that the register has been short a few times since."

"You did the right thing to not pursue it," he said. "Don't bring up the money with anyone at the pizzeria again, alright? Write down Billy's full name and address for me, and I'll see if I can find anything on him."

"Are you sure? I don't want to distract you from… other cases."

"Taking a break to look into something like this will be good for me. Sometimes it's best to take a step back and let your subconscious work on a problem for a while. There is such a thing as being too close to a case."

She wondered if he was thinking of his wife's murder. She was itching to ask him about it, but couldn't bring herself to form the words. They had gone on this outing to escape the oppressive atmosphere in town. They didn't need to talk about yet another sad subject.

"Alright," she said. "I'll get you his information, then try to put it out of my mind. He really is a good employee. If it wasn't for the money that Jacob found, I wouldn't have any reason to suspect him. I could be completely mistaken. Billy seems like a good kid."

She was glad that she had shared her concerns with Russell. With any luck, he'd get back to her in a day or two with good news about Billy, and she could put the whole matter out of her mind once and for all.

CHAPTER TWELVE

Ellie felt refreshed after her boating trip with Russell. Maybe her grandmother had been right; there was something to be said for making time for oneself. The memories of finding Jason's body still weighed on her, but she felt better able to cope with it. She was thankful that she had gotten there before his wife. While she didn't think she would ever be able to stop seeing the image of his body lying on the floor whenever she closed her eyes, she knew that it would have been a hundred times worse for his wife to have been the one to find him.

She got to the pizzeria early the next day, excited for the first time in days at the prospect of designing a new pizza for the weekly special. She wanted to do something inspired by the spring weather. She pulled out her phone and searched online for ideas. One of the first things that came up when she typed in the word "spring" was spring rolls. That was just the inspiration that she was looking for.

Why not do a spring roll inspired pizza? she thought. The spring rolls from her favorite Chinese takeout place in the next town over were light, but bursting with flavor. It shouldn't be too hard to translate something similar to pizza form. It would probably work best with a thin crust, and of course she would need some sort of sauce to pull everything together.

A few minutes later, Ellie was ready to put her freshly formed plan into motion. She had never made her own peanut sauce before, but knew that there would be no better time like the present to try. The first problem was that she simply didn't have many of the ingredients. Things like peanut butter, soy sauce, and sesame oil generally had no place in a pizzeria. She checked the time. She might have just enough time to run to the grocery store, pick up the ingredients she didn't have, and make a test pizza before opening, but if the new pizza wasn't any good she wouldn't have the time to try anything else.

I've got to take some risks, or I won't ever get anywhere, she thought. As far as risks went, this one was pretty small; she doubted that many of her customers would notice if they didn't have a new weekly special on the board today.

An hour later, Ellie slid the test pizza into the over. Homemade spicy peanut sauce — she had made a mild version, too, for those who didn't care for spicy foods — shredded carrots, red and green bell peppers, and crushed peanuts made up the toppings. When the pizza came out, she would add cilantro, scallions, and a drizzle of olive oil to tie it all together. She could already tell that this pizza was going to be a success. It wasn't quite a traditional pizza, but it looked and smelled fantastic. Hopefully her customers would be brave enough to try it.

The employee entrance opened just as she set the timer on the stove. She looked around to see Billy and Iris come in. Both of them were laughing, but quieted down when they saw her.

"Oh, hi Ms. Pacelli," Iris said. "I forgot you were going to be here to open this morning. I guess we didn't have to come in this early."

"The more the merrier," Ellie said. "I just put a pizza in the oven. You two can be my taste testers when it comes out."

"What kind is it?"

"It's a spring roll pizza with spicy peanut sauce."

"That sounds… interesting," Billy said.

"It's a bit different," Ellie admitted. "But I think it will be good. Doing something new once in a while can't hurt."

While she waited for the pizza to cook, she cleaned up her work station and took the garbage out to the dumpster. On her way back in, she noticed that there was only one car in the lot; Billy's. She went back inside with a frown on her face. *How did Iris get here?* she wondered. She got her chance to ask the young woman that very question when Billy stepped out of the kitchen to go turn the restaurant's sign on.

"How did you get here? I noticed that your car isn't in the lot."

"Sorry, it's in the shop. Billy gave me a ride."

"Oh, that's fine, I was just curious. It's nice out, I figured you might have walked."

She kept her eye on Iris and Billy as they tried the pizza together and then finished the morning routines. Was it all in her imagination, or did they seem to be flirting? Yes, she was sure that Iris had just brushed his arm on her way by on purpose.

Could that be why he didn't touch the money that I left out? she wondered. *If they are dating, Iris might have felt obliged to tell him about what we suspected. That means that he really might be stealing, and he's just been hiding it well.*

She didn't get a chance to confront the young woman with her questions; the pizzeria was officially open, and the first customers were already streaming in.

CHAPTER THIRTEEN

The spring roll pizza was a hit. Ellie and Iris had a hard time keeping up with the orders. Billy was busy driving back and forth from Papa Pacelli's to the delivery addresses. The three of them made a good team, which just made the pizzeria owner even sadder when she thought about the possibility that Billy was stealing from her — or worse, her customers. Russell still hadn't gotten back to her with results from that background search he had run. She didn't blame him; he was busy enough as it was with the case of the Kittiport serial killer hanging over his head.

"I might have been safer if I had stayed in Chicago," she muttered to herself as she rolled out the dough. She chuckled. "I never thought I would say that."

"What'd you say, Ms. P.?" Iris asked, pausing on her way through the kitchen door to look back at her boss.

"Sorry, just talking to myself, Iris," Ellie said. "Do you want to switch once I get this pizza in the oven? You've been rushing back and forth for a while now."

"Yeah, I could use a drink and a chance to sit for a second," her employee said with a grin. "We've been doing pretty well lately, huh?"

"We sure have."

With an unusual rush of emotion for the deceased grandfather that she had barely known, Ellie found herself wishing that Arthur Pacelli was alive to see his restaurant now. She was sure he would be proud of it, and proud of her.

She was glad for the chance to switch with Iris. She enjoyed cooking, but she also liked to be out with the customers and see how they were faring. Any complaints about the food or drinks, she could handle on the spot. She didn't hesitate to give discounts if someone seemed unhappy. The pizzeria's reputation was important to her. Sales would go up and down, but their reputation as a quality, family friendly restaurant shouldn't waver.

The bell by the front door jingled as someone pushed it open. She looked up just as the three newcomers reached the register. *I know her,* she realized with shock. The woman that she recognized was Nancy, the wife of one of the dead men. The other two women only looked vaguely familiar to her. She knew that they must have come to Papa Pacelli's in the past, but she couldn't remember their names.

"How can I help you?" she asked, trying not to stare at Nancy. How was the woman faring since her husband's death? How was their child handling it? She knew it really wasn't any of her business, but since she had been the one to find the body, she felt connected to Jason's murder more than the others.

"We'd like three personal pizzas, two lemonades, and a soda," one of the other women said. They took turns giving her their orders. She hurried into the kitchen to relay the order so Iris could work on getting it into the oven, grabbed their drinks, and delivered the tray to their table. She must have looked at Nancy for a second too long, because the woman spoke up.

"Hey, don't I know you?"

"If you've been here before, you've probably seen me," Ellie said. She extended a hand. "Eleanora Pacelli. Owner and manager of Papa Pacelli's Pizzeria, the best pizza joint in town."

Nancy shook hands with her. A second later, her eyes went wide. "Oh, I know where I remember you from. It's not from here. You're the one who found my husband, aren't you?"

Ellie nodded. She felt bad. She hadn't meant to bring up memories of that horrible evening. The poor woman was just there to have lunch with her friends.

"I'm so glad I found you," said Nancy, much to her surprise. "I knew that one of the delivery drivers from this place was the one who found him, but I didn't see much of you except your hair and car. I… well, I wasn't exactly in my right mind just then."

"Why did you want to find me?" Ellie asked, confused.

"To ask you questions, of course." She looked around at her companions, and they both nodded in agreement. "Three weeks ago, we were all married women. Today we are all widows. We want to know why."

The three women managed to convince Ellie to join them for lunch. She hesitated only out of concern for Iris, who was working the kitchen by herself. Her curiosity won out in the end, and she made a mental promise to tear herself away from the women if it got any busier in the pizzeria.

"I have to warn you," she said. "I probably don't know anything more than you ladies do. I called the police as soon as I realized what had happened, and they took it from there."

"I know," Nancy said. "But we just needed to talk to you, you know? You're the closest thing to a witness that we could find. The police don't seem to have a clue what's going on. I just want to find out what happened to my husband."

The other two women nodded. They had introduced themselves as Kari and Maria. Ellie tried to remember which was which, but they both looked similar with their dark hair and black mourning clothes.

"So, can you think of anything odd you might have seen on your way there?" Nancy asked. "Did any of the vehicles you passed stand out to you? We figure the killer must be someone we know, so we might be able to recognize their car if you describe it."

"I don't remember any of the vehicles I passed on my way to the delivery," Ellie said. "And I didn't see anyone driving around the suburb either. I didn't even realize that something was wrong until I was almost on the porch. I'm sorry."

One of the other two women — she was pretty sure it was Maria — spoke up. "Andy was acting weird for a couple of days before he died. He was being secretive, which was pretty unusual for him, and some of my favorite jewelry went missing. I thought he might have been seeing another woman. In fact, I was going to confront him about it the night that he died."

"Did you tell that to the sheriff?" Ellie asked.

"It didn't occur to me that it might be related at first, and then I was worried that telling them might make it look like I killed him out of jealousy. I didn't want to risk getting arrested for something I didn't do. Devon, my twelve-year-old, needs me. He can't be left with no one at such a young age."

"The thing is," Nancy said, "Jason was acting oddly, too. And Kari told me at work that her Trevor was sneaking out at night behind her back."

This jogged something in Ellie's memory. "Wait, don't the three of you work together?"

All three women raised their eyebrows. "How did you know that?" Nancy asked.

"I'm friends with the sheriff," she explained. "And his sister-in-law is my best friend. I picked up bits and pieces. Where do you work?"

"The bar in town," Nancy said. "We met through work, but have been friends outside of work for a while now."

"Our husbands didn't know each other well," Kari chimed in. "Well, Trevor never spent time with the other two. I guess Andy and Jason might have known each other."

"They did," Nancy confirmed. "But they didn't get along at all." She slid her eyes over to Maria and flushed before saying, "And I admit, at first I thought Jason might have had something to do with Andy's death. They had gotten into an argument earlier in the day."

Ellie was still trying to put all of the bits and pieces together. The wives all worked together, that just couldn't be a coincidence. Or could it? And all three of the women said that their husbands had been acting strangely before their deaths. Maybe someone at the bar had been killing them, someone dangerously obsessed with the three women.

"I think you should tell all of this to the police," she said. "And I mean all of it, without worrying how it looks."

None of the three women met her gaze. Nancy sighed before she spoke again. "Look, the sheriff has already questioned each of us. He thinks we might have had something to do with our husbands' deaths. I have a kid; Maria has a kid… they have to be our priorities right now. Devon needs his mom to be there for him, and if the police think we might have had a reason to want to get rid of our husbands, then best case scenario, I have to deal with a bunch of lawyers and hassle before it gets cleared up. I'm not putting Brian through that, not when he just lost his dad."

Ellie nodded. She wasn't sure she agreed with the other woman's reasoning, but she understood it. In the mother's eyes, she was putting her child first.

"I'm sorry," she said. "I can't help you. I told the police everything I know. If I remembered anything else, I would have called them and told them right away."

"I understand," Nancy said, but Ellie thought she looked disappointed.

"One more thing," Maria said. "Did you ever see any of our husbands in here, with women that weren't us?"

She thought back, trying to match the pictures of the men she had seen in the obituary with her customers, but there were just too many people coming through the pizzeria on a daily basis for her to be sure.

"I can't remember," she said apologetically. "I spend a lot of time in the kitchen, so I'm not as familiar with the regulars as I could be. I wish I could help you, but I can't."

With that, she got up and left the women to eat their meal in peace. She had a lot to think about, and there was one person that she was just itching to share it all with.

CHAPTER FOURTEEN

B y the time the pizzeria closed that evening, Ellie was beat. As she swept out the dining area, she toyed with the idea of going straight home, but knew that she wouldn't be able to sleep until she told Russell all about her conversation with the wives of the murdered men today. She had to admit, she had been impressed by the women. They were doing what they could to figure out who had killed their husbands. It couldn't have been easy for any of them, but she especially felt for the ones who had children. She had forgone that part of life, and could hardly imagine what it must be like to be so completely responsible for another human being. And those poor kids, growing up without fathers… whoever the killer was, he or she deserved to rot in prison for a very, very long time.

After closing up, she drove over to her favorite coffee shop and ordered two drinks before heading to the sheriff's department. For

Christmas, she had bought the department a new coffee maker, but even so, nothing compared to the caramel mochas from the little shop.

She had texted the sheriff a few minutes before close, so he knew she was coming. He met her at the door and took his coffee gratefully.

"My favorite," he said. "This ought to hold off the sleep deprivation for another hour or two."

"You know what would fix it completely?" she asked. "More sleep."

"You make it sound so easy." He leaned down to give her a quick kiss, then held the door for her so she could go in. It was late, and the secretary, Ms. Lafferre, had already gone home.

"I guess I'm here because I knew I wouldn't be able to sleep myself. We're a pair of insomniacs."

"Perfectly matched, then," he said. "So, what was it you wanted to tell me? You said it had to do with the murder cases?"

"Yes. You'll never guess who came into the pizzeria today…"

She told him all about her lunch with the three women. She didn't leave any detail out. If they weren't going to tell the sheriff the full truth, then she would. She hadn't made any promises to keep her mouth shut, and she hadn't even asked for the women to talk to her in the first place. Russell couldn't do his job right if he didn't know everything. If someone else died, and she hadn't told him everything that the women had told her, she would never be able to forgive herself.

"All of the men were acting this way?" He shook his head. "That's just… odd."

"I've been trying to figure it out all day," she admitted. "One of the men might have been having an affair, but what are the chances that all three would have been?"

"Their deaths keep getting more and more mysterious," he said. "There are so many clues, but none of them seem to tie together. The fact that the three women work together is still bothering me as well. There just has to be something I'm missing."

"I hate this so much. I feel terrible for the women, and their children, and the men who died, of course. I feel scared to be home alone, and whenever I leave my grandmother home alone, I'm terrified of what I might come back to. So far all of the victims have been men, but what if the next one isn't? Or what if next time it's someone I know, like you or James?"

"Come here." He put his coffee down and wrapped her in a hug. "I'd be happy if the killer came to my door. At least then I could quit looking for him. I don't think you have anything to worry about. Right now, the women, and that bar, are the two things that tie all three men together. Unless I'm completely wrong about all of this, there was something going on that we just aren't aware of yet. It will all fall into place eventually."

"I hope you're right." She closed her eyes and rested her head against his shoulder for a moment before popping them open again. "Hey, didn't you say you had something interesting to tell me, too?"

"I do." He grimaced. "It's not exactly good news. It's about Billy."

"Oh no, did you find some sort of criminal record on him?"

He nodded. "He's been arrested for petty theft a couple of times, and once for facilitating illegal gambling."

"That means he lied on his application," she said, stung. "I can't believe it. And Iris… I wonder what she has to do with all of it."

"Iris?" he said. "She's the one with the brightly colored hair, isn't she?"

Ellie nodded. "They drove to work together today, and I watched them flirt all afternoon. There's definitely something going on between them."

"I don't think she would cover up for him if he was stealing, do you?" Russell asked, a frown causing his brows to crease. "She can't have known him long. Why would she risk jeopardizing her job for someone she just met?"

"I don't know," Ellie said. "I really don't. I just want this whole thing with Billy to be over. Should I fire him tomorrow? No, I should get him to confess first, shouldn't I? Otherwise he'll just go and steal from someone else. He must be taking money from more than just the pizzeria. He had a lot of cash in that backpack of his."

"Slow down," the sheriff said. "You can't go confronting this guy. He might get dangerous if he thinks you're on to him."

"I can't in good conscience let him go get some other job in town if I know he's a thief. He'd still be stealing from the same people, he'd just be doing it from some other restaurant," she said.

Maybe he could go and work at Cheesaroni Calzones, she thought. *They sure deserve someone like him.* She knew that she wouldn't really be comfortable with that. In the end, he would still be stealing from the people of Kittiport. She frowned, thinking of the customer's wallet that she had found. That was what made her the maddest of all. Stealing petty cash from the register was one thing. Stealing a wallet from a customer was a whole different ballgame.

"If you're set on outing him, I have an idea," Russell said. "But you have to promise to do exactly what I say…"

CHAPTER FIFTEEN

I t was a couple of days until the shifts at the pizzeria lined up just right for Russell and Ellie to put their plan into action. She got to the pizzeria a good hour before it opened and began her preparations as usual, trying to ignore her rapidly beating heart and sweaty palms. This was exciting. It was like being undercover, except she was really just being herself. She wondered what Billy was thinking as he drove over. Was he nervous? Did he know something was up? Or had he believed her when she said she just wanted to talk to him? Now that she knew he had a history of stealing, she had no doubts that he was the one taking small amounts of cash out of the register. It made her angry to think that she had given him a chance, and even after knowing her history with the previous manager, he had decided to take advantage of her. Today, she would get the truth once and for all.

The employee door opened, and in walked Billy, just on time as he almost always was. He did look a little nervous. *Serves him right,* she thought.

"Hi, Billy. Come and sit down with me. Feel free to pour yourself a glass of lemonade first, if you would like."

He shook his head and joined her at the round staff table in the kitchen immediately. "Did I do something wrong, Ms. P.?"

"I just need to ask you a few things," she said. "I've noticed that the register has been short pretty often lately. And I can't help but notice that it always happens on the evenings that you work. I don't want to sound like I'm accusing you of anything, I'm just wondering if you have any idea what's going on." It was difficult to stay polite when she already knew that he was a liar and a thief, but she thought she was doing a pretty good job.

"I have no idea," he said, his eyes widening in surprise. "How much are we talking here? If it's just a few pennies, I may have made a mistake while counting."

She was prepared for this. She handed him a printout, with the differences between what should have been in the drawer and what was actually in the drawer highlighted.

He looked at it for a few seconds before glancing back up at her with obvious embarrassment on his face. "These are the exact amount I've been taking out in tips each night," he said. "I must have been doing it wrong."

She frowned. She hadn't expected this. "Let's look at the receipts."

She got up and pulled the receipt box out from the pantry. It wasn't as organized as it should have been, but it didn't take her long to pull the receipts from the past few days off the top of the haphazard pile. Sure enough, when she crunched the numbers, the amount missing from the drawer each night matched the tips on the receipts from each of the pizzas Billy had delivered.

"Jacob showed me how to cash out each evening and grab the tips that people left with a card. I just must have missed a step somewhere."

"It sure looks like that," she said, somewhat reluctantly. She had been prepared to fire him the second he had admitted to stealing, but it looked now like he hadn't been stealing from her at all. "Wait here for —"

She was cut off as the employee door opened once again, revealing Iris. Ellie frowned. What was the young woman doing there? She wasn't scheduled to work that day, and even if she had been, it was way too early for her to be there.

"Ms. P..." Her voice trailed off as her eyes landed on Billy. It took her just an instant to rephrase whatever it was that she had been about to say. "Can I talk to you, Ms. P.? It's important."

"Not right now, Iris, I'm in the middle of a conversation with Billy."

"It's about that thing we were talking about..." Her eyes flicked to Billy again. "Um, my medical problem."

Ellie blinked. What medical problem was the girl talking about? She didn't remember Iris telling her anything about any issues.

Whatever it was, it must have been important, or Iris wouldn't have been so adamant about interrupting.

"Alright, Billy will you wait here? I'll talk to Iris in the other room really quickly."

Feeling annoyed at her employee, she gestured Iris over and walked through the swinging door that led to the dining area. Russell was waiting on the other side. When Iris saw him, she gave a small jump, but to her credit didn't make a peep. Ellie made sure the door was shut completely before speaking to Iris in a whisper.

"What's going on?" she asked. "First, are you okay?"

"What — oh, yeah. I was just trying to get you to talk to me. Sorry about that."

"What's so important that it couldn't wait?"

"It's about Billy. I don't know if you noticed, but I've been spending more time with him lately."

"I noticed," Ellie said.

"Right, well I've been trying to get close enough to him that he would tell me where he got all of his money from."

"Oh." Ellie shot an embarrassed look towards Russell. It looked like she had been wrong about her youngest employee. "I have to apologize, Iris, I thought that you might have told him about the test money we set out."

"I would never, but I can see why you might have thought that. It's fine, it doesn't matter, because he's not stealing from the pizzeria."

"I just figured that out," the pizzeria owner said. "He had just been making a mistake with the register. He was only taking his tips out." Behind Iris, she saw Russell sigh.

"I don't know about that, but I do know where he got all of that money. He's been gambling, Ms. P.! He takes money from people all around town. And guess what, he even told me that he makes stops sometimes while he's driving to collect. That's why he's late occasionally."

Russell frowned. Ellie thought he was going to say something, but when he remained silent, she said, "Wow, thank you for telling me, Iris."

"He said he takes bets on sports at some bar in town, and he sometimes makes a few thousand in a night. He doesn't even need this job, not really."

Iris's words felt like a punch in Ellie's gut. *He takes bets at a bar in town... this is a one bar kind of town. He's taking those bets at the same bar where Nancy and her friends work. The same bar that all three of those men must have frequented.* She met Russell's eyes over her employee's shoulder, and knew that he must have realized the same thing. This was the link that he had needed to solve the case.

CHAPTER SIXTEEN

B illy opened the door from the kitchen. Ellie started. Russell, who was standing just on the other side of the door, froze. If Billy looked to just slightly to his left, he would see the sheriff.

"Did you need anything else, Ms. P.? Or is it okay if I go? I've still got about half an hour before my shift is supposed to start."

"Um, I'm not done talking to you yet, Billy. Please wait."

He sighed and shut the door. She breathed out a sigh of relief. Their cover had almost been blown.

Turning to Iris, she said, "Thank you so much for telling me. I really appreciate it. You have no idea how much. Was there anything else?"

"Nope," Iris said. "I just thought you should know."

"Thank you," she said again. "Go enjoy your day off, now. I'll take care of Billy."

Iris nodded and left, leaving Ellie and Russell alone in the main room of the pizzeria. The sheriff was still frowning.

"I'm going to go talk to him," she said.

"Ellie, no. He might be the one who killed those men. It's far too dangerous."

"Are you going to arrest him?"

He gritted his teeth. "I can't yet. I need evidence, not just hearsay. She didn't even say anything to tie him to those poor men."

"Then I'm going to go talk to him. You listen at the door like you were. It's the same plan as before."

"Except now you're in there with a killer, not just a thief."

"If he's guilty, then I've been around a killer for weeks. I just didn't know it. How is this any different?"

Satisfied that she had won the argument, she went back into the kitchen without waiting for his reply. Billy was lounging at the table, spinning his phone around with one hand.

"Is Iris okay?" he asked, looking up.

"She's fine," Ellie said. "We can get back to our discussion now."

"I thought we got that cleared up? I didn't steal anything, and now I know how to do tips right so I won't mess it up again."

"There are still other things to discuss."

"Like what?"

"Like —" for an instant, she almost mentioned the bag full of money that she had seen. She cast around for another excuse to keep him there longer. Her eyes landed on the sink. "Like the dishes."

"The dishes?"

"Yes. I think you've been using too much soap. It might seem silly, but it adds up, and it also leaves soap residue on the dishes. The customers complain."

She reached for one of the heavy ceramic plates to show him, but her hands were shaking. The plate slipped out of her grip and shattered on the floor. Out of the corner of her eye, she saw the swinging door that led to the main area twitch open a fraction of an inch. The thought of Russell watching over her calmed her down.

"Why are you acting so weird, Ms. Pacelli?" he asked. "What did Iris say to you?"

"Nothing, I just haven't eaten breakfast. Why, is there something you don't want her to say?"

She met his eyes and was surprised by how cold and uncaring his gaze was. What had happened to the charming young man that she had hired?

"There's plenty I'd rather you didn't know about me, Ms. Pacelli," he said. "But that doesn't matter, does it? Because this whole thing was a set-up from the beginning, wasn't it?"

The door to the kitchen swung open at the same instant that Billy stood up and pointed a gun at her. His eyes never left her face, even when Russell shouted at him to drop the weapon.

"I don't think so, dude. How about you put yours down?"

"How did you know he was here?" Ellie gasped. Their plan had seemed so perfect. How had she ended up at gunpoint?

"I saw Iris glance at something on the other side of the door when I opened it. Then I saw the door move when you dropped that dish. I put two and two together quickly enough."

"Billy, that's enough. Put the firearm on the table and come over here with your hands up," Russell said, his voice dangerous.

"Yeah, I'm not an idiot. I don't want to spend the rest of my life in some cell. If I even see your finger twitch, your girlfriend is gone. Then where will you get your free pizzas, Sheriff? No, I'm just going to walk out of here nice and slow."

Billy started inching towards the employee door. Ellie's eyes darted around as she looked for something she could use to defend herself, but there was nothing. Why did she keep the kitchen so darn clean? Russell caught her gaze and shook his head slightly. He didn't want her to try anything, so she wouldn't, no matter how hard it was to make herself obey the young man who was pointing a gun at her.

"You, Ms. Pacelli, move so you're standing between me and him. I don't want him trying to get a shot off at me."

Russell nodded, so she did as she was told, gritting her teeth the entire time.

"And face me, I don't want the two of you communicating where I can't see."

She turned around. He was almost at the door now. She tensed. If she dropped to the floor, Russell might be able to get off a shot before Billy could aim at her.

"Did you kill them?" she asked. "I just don't understand, Billy. Why?"

"I came to collect, and they didn't have enough to pay up. One smart guy just threw his wallet at me from an upstairs window. I let him slide. I like it when people throw bank cards and cash at me," he said simply. "You want to know the funny part? You paid me to kill them. I stopped at their houses after I delivered the pizzas. The murders were all on your dime."

"I would never have —"

"No more talking, you're just trying to stall. I know this tactic. Everyone always tries to stall. It didn't help those men, why would it help you?"

The young man reached the door and nudged it open, never taking his eyes off of her. She had no doubt that he would shoot if she gave him reason, and the thought of possibly dying today in the pizzeria's kitchen was enough to keep her from acting.

"Don't worry, sheriff, I'm getting out of town and not coming back. You won't hear from me again, though Iris might. I can't believe that b—"

His final words were cut off. Ellie saw a strong arm wrap around his neck in a choke hold. Billy raised the gun and tried to aim it behind himself at his assailant, but before he could get off a shot, his body jolted and he fell to the ground, half in and half out of the door.

Ellie was still frozen in shock, gaping at the scene in front of her. A familiar red-haired face appeared in the doorway.

"Sorry," Liam said. "I interrupted him, but he didn't seem to have anything constructive to say, anyway. I was worried he might try to shoot Ellie as he left, to distract you. I couldn't let that happen. Bethany here tazed him, but a young man like him won't be down long. Ellie, you okay?"

She nodded. Liam crouched down to handcuff the limp man. Russell came up behind her and touched her shoulder.

"Are you really okay?" he asked in a low voice, his whiskers tickling her ear. She nodded again, not trusting herself to speak. She felt on the verge of hysteria, and didn't know if she would laugh or cry if she opened her mouth. Not one, but three, murders had just been solved. The murderer had turned out to be one of her own employees. It was all too overwhelming.

She felt Russell take her hand. Without thinking, she said, "I love you."

He was silent for a second. She didn't dare look over. It had just slipped out. She felt heat rise to her face. What had she been thinking? Then his hand tightened on hers.

"I love you, too."